Little Lord Fauntleroy

Retold from the Frances Hodgson Burnett
original by Eva Mason

Illustrated by Troy Howell

STERLING

New York / London
www.sterlingpublishing.com/kids

STERLING and the distinctive Sterling logo
are registered trademarks of Sterling Publishing Co., Inc.

Library of Congress Cataloging-in-Publication Data

Mason, Eva.
  Little Lord Fauntleroy / retold from the Frances Hodgson Burnett original;
abridged by Eva Mason; illustrated by Troy Howell; afterword by Arthur Pober.
      p. cm. — (Classic starts)
  Summary: An abridged retelling of the story of an American boy who goes to
live with his grandfather in England where he becomes heir to a title and a
fortune.
  ISBN-13: 978-1-4027-4578-2
  ISBN-10: 1-4027-4578-8
  [1. Grandfathers—Fiction. 2. England—Fiction.] I. Howell, Troy ill. II. Burnett,
Frances Hodgson, 1849–1924. Little Lord Fauntleroy. III. Title.

PZ7.M387Lit 2007
[Fic]—dc22

                                                                    2007003637

2 4 6 8 10 9 7 5 3 1

Published by Sterling Publishing Co., Inc.
387 Park Avenue South, New York, NY 10016
Copyright © 2008 by Eva Mason
Illustrations copyright © 2008 by Troy Howell
Distributed in Canada by Sterling Publishing
^c/o Canadian Manda Group, 165 Dufferin Street,
Toronto, Ontario, Canada M6K 3H6
Distributed in the United Kingdom by GMC Distribution Services,
Castle Place, 166 High Street, Lewes, East Sussex, England BN7 1XU
Distributed in Australia by Capricorn Link (Australia) Pty. Ltd.
P.O. Box 704, Windsor, NSW 2756, Australia

Classic Starts is a trademark of Sterling Publishing Co., Inc.

Sterling ISBN-13: 978-1-4027-4578-2
ISBN-10: 1-4027-4578-8

For information about custom editions, special sales, premium and
corporate purchases, please contact Sterling Special Sales
Department at 800-805-5489 or specialsales@sterlingpublishing.com.

CONTENTS

❦

CHAPTER 1

A Great Surprise

∽

"Dearest," Cedric said to his mama. "Dearest, is my papa better?" Cedric called his mama Dearest, just like his papa had.

Cedric's papa had been terribly ill, and Cedric had been sent away until he got better. But when the boy returned, he found Dearest sitting in her chair by the window. She was dressed in black, and her pretty face looked very sad.

Cedric went to her. He felt her arms tremble. There was something in her face that made his heart beat fast with worry.

"Dearest," he said again quietly, "is Papa well?"

Suddenly he knew what to do. He wrapped his arms around her neck, and he kissed her again and again. She put her face on his shoulder and started sobbing. She was holding on to him tightly, as if she would never let go.

"Yes, he is well," Dearest said at last. "But we—we have no one left but each other."

Cedric was only a little boy, but somehow he understood. His big, handsome papa was not coming back. He was dead.

∽

A few years passed. Dearest cried whenever he asked about his papa, so Cedric secretly decided not to talk about him.

He remembered a few things about his papa. His name was Captain Cedric Errol. He was very tall and had blue eyes and a mustache. Cedric remembered how wonderful it felt when his papa carried him around on his shoulders. That's what Cedric remembered most.

He also knew that his papa was not from New York, where he and Dearest lived. His papa was from England.

Cedric thought that was why his papa's family never visited. They were too far away. His mama's family never visited either, but that was because she had no family. She was an orphan.

Before Dearest married his papa, she had worked for a rich old lady who was not kind to her. One day, Captain Errol was visiting the old lady's house and noticed Cedric's mama running up the stairs. From that moment on, the captain couldn't stop thinking about her. She looked so sweet, so innocent. He came back to visit again and again. He fell in love with her, and soon— quicker than anyone could have guessed—they were planning to get married.

This marriage made some people very unhappy, even angry. The captain's father was especially upset. He was the Earl of Dorincourt, a rich and important nobleman who lived in a fine, beautiful castle. He was known for having a terrible temper. He also hated America and Americans.

The earl had two sons who were older than Captain Cedric. The oldest son was a lord. He would one day become the Earl of Dorincourt, after the old earl died. If the first son died, the second son would become the earl's heir. As for the third son, he would only become a lord if both of his brothers died. More than likely, he would never be the Earl of Dorincourt. He would never even be very rich, since most of the family fortune would go to his older brothers.

Captain Cedric knew this, but it didn't matter to him. He was a kind young man, and very handsome. He was also brave and generous. Everyone loved him. His older brothers were not handsome or kind or smart. They wasted their time and money and had very few real friends.

The earl's two older sons were a disappointment. They embarrassed him. His heirs were not an honor to his noble name.

The earl thought it was the worst of luck that his third son had all the gifts. The beauty and the charm and the smarts—these should have gone

5

to the son who would one day become Earl of Dorincourt. On his third son, these qualities were wasted.

The earl hated comparing his third son to the older brothers. His presence was a constant reminder of their failures. And so the earl sent his third son far away, to America. That way, the old earl wouldn't have to see him and be reminded of his other sons' faults.

Six months passed, and the earl became lonely. He didn't say it out loud, but he missed his youngest son. He wrote Captain Cedric a letter and asked him to come home.

At the same time, Captain Cedric wrote his father a letter. He told him of the sweet, pretty American girl he wanted to marry. He asked his father for his blessing.

But he didn't get it. When the earl received the letter, he was furious. For a whole hour, he raged around his castle like a tiger. Then he sat down and wrote a nasty response: Captain Cedric was never to come home again. He was not to write to his father or his brothers. He could live however he wanted. He could die wherever he wanted. He would be cut off from his family forever. And he would never get help from his father for as long as he lived.

The captain was heartbroken. At first, he didn't know what to do. He had no work experience, but he did have courage, and he wouldn't give up. He soon found a job in New York and married the girl he loved.

His new life was very different from the one he had known in England. But he was young and full of hope. He rented a small, humble house on a quiet street. It was a happy home—it was where he lived with his new wife, and where his son was born. The captain was never once sorry for what he did.

His little boy, Cedric, was sweet and charming.

He had curly golden hair and big brown eyes with impossibly long eyelashes. He was very handsome.

The boy was also friendly and well-mannered. When he was out on the street, he smiled at strangers and looked them straight in the eye. He talked to everyone, asking after their business, their health, and their family. People found him to be quite amusing. His greatest friend was the groceryman on the corner, Mr. Hobbs, who was known as the grumpiest man around. But Cedric could make even Mr. Hobbs smile.

Cedric had a kind heart and was quick to understand other people's feelings. This may have been because he never heard a mean word at home. He had always been loved and treated tenderly. He had always heard his mama called by pretty, loving names, and so he used them himself when he spoke to her. And he had always seen his papa watch over his mama, so he made sure to take good care of her, too.

So when Cedric learned that his papa wasn't coming back, and he saw how sad Dearest was, he knew that he needed to make her happy.

He climbed up on her knees, kissed her, and put his head on her shoulder. He brought her toys and picture books to show her. When she lay down on the sofa, he curled up quietly at her side until she woke up and talked with him again. He was a greater comfort to her than he realized.

"Oh, Mary," he heard her say once to her faithful housekeeper and maid, "I know he is trying to help me. He looks at me sometimes with this curious little look, as if he knows how my heart feels. As if he is sorry for me. Then he shows me something to put my mind on other things. He is such a little man already."

Cedric always acted older than his years. He

learned to read when he was very little. He would lie on the rug in the evenings and read aloud— sometimes stories, and other times big books that grown-ups would read. Sometimes he even read the newspaper.

Cedric didn't know what all the big words meant, but he sounded them out and asked for help with the stranger spellings. He was especially interested in politics. Dearest and Mary would laugh in delight at the funny things he would say.

Mary was fond of Cedric. She had been helping his mother ever since he was born. She was proud of how graceful he was and of his fine manners. She especially adored his bright curly hair, which fell just past his ears.

Mary liked to sew him small suits that made him look like a tiny gentleman. "You look like a young lord," she would tell him. And Cedric would laugh, and be a little confused. He didn't think he looked like a young lord. He didn't even know what a lord was.

Cedric thought Mr. Hobbs was a very rich and powerful person, like a lord, he supposed. Mr. Hobbs had so many things in his store—prunes and figs and oranges and biscuits—and he had a horse and a wagon. Cedric was fond of the milk-man and the baker and the shoe-shine boy and the apple-woman who worked near the park, but he liked Mr. Hobbs the best. He would visit the grocery store every day, and pull up a stool to talk to Mr. Hobbs.

And they would talk for hours, the grumpy grocery-man and the sweet seven-year-old boy who had lost his father.

It was quite surprising how many things Cedric and Mr. Hobbs found to talk about—the Fourth of July, for instance. They could talk about the American Day of Independence for a long time. Mr. Hobbs had a very bad opinion

of the British. He said they were great villains.
What he liked were the patriotic heroes of
America. He would even recite parts of the
Declaration of Independence, and Cedric would
get so excited that his heart would beat fast
when he listened.

One day when Cedric was visiting Mr. Hobbs,
a very odd thing happened. They were talking
about England and the queen. Mr. Hobbs said
that he did not like the English royalty. He did
not like earls or dukes, and he was being very
stubborn about it.

"Did you ever know any dukes, Mr. Hobbs?"
Cedric asked. "Or earls?"

"In fact, I did not," said Mr. Hobbs. "But I
don't like them!"

"Maybe they wouldn't be earls if they knew
any better," said Cedric, starting to feel bad for the
earls and the dukes.

"Wouldn't they!" said Mr. Hobbs. "They just love it! It's all they want! They're a bad lot."

Cedric and Mr. Hobbs were in the middle of this conversation when Mary appeared. Cedric thought that maybe she had come to buy some sugar, but she said that wasn't it. Her eyes were shining, like she was excited about something.

"Come home, darlin'," she said to Cedric. "The mistress is wantin' you."

Cedric slipped down from his stool. "Good-bye, Mr. Hobbs," he said. "We'll talk more about the earls and dukes tomorrow."

Mary was staring at him, shaking her head.

"What's the matter, Mary? Has the sun given Dearest a headache?" Cedric asked anxiously.

But Mary said it was not that. Cedric rushed home with her, feeling nervous. When they reached the house, there was a fancy carriage outside. Someone was in the little parlor talking to Dearest.

Mary wouldn't let Cedric go into the parlor just yet. Instead, she hurried him upstairs to put on his best summer suit, the cream-colored one with the red belt. She told him to find his best shoes, too.

When he was dressed at last, he ran down into the parlor. The visitor was a tall, thin old gentleman with a sharp, serious face. He was sitting in an armchair.

Dearest was standing nearby with a pale face. There were tears in her eyes.

"Oh, Ceddie!" she cried. She ran to him and held him in her arms.

The tall old gentleman rose from his chair and looked deeply at Cedric for a long while. He didn't seem displeased.

"And so," he finally said, "this is little Lord Fauntleroy."

CHAPTER 2

Cedric's Friends

⌒♱

Cedric was stunned at the news. His grand-father, whom he had never seen, was an earl. Both of his uncles would have been earls, too, but they had died. His father would have been an earl if *he* hadn't died. And now, since only Cedric was left, *he* was to be an earl one day. Now he was to be called by the family name, Lord Fauntleroy. And he would have to go live in England.

"Dearest," he said, "I'd rather not go all the way to England. Must I go?"

"I'm sorry, Ceddie," Dearest said, "But, yes, you must. I know your papa would wish you to go. He loved his home. I would be selfish if I didn't send you."

Cedric didn't understand. He would miss his home and his friends. When Mr. Havisham— his grandfather's lawyer—had come to Cedric's house, the little boy had heard many exciting things. But it didn't make him feel any better to know that he would be a rich man when he grew up. He would have castles here and castles there. He would have tenants who lived on his lands, whatever that meant. But right now, he still had to leave his home and his friends.

Cedric was especially troubled about leaving Mr. Hobbs. He went as soon as he could to tell him the news.

Cedric knew that Mr. Hobbs didn't like earls. They had just been talking about it. So Cedric was very nervous when he said, "I am one — or I am going to be. I cannot lie to you."

Mr. Hobbs was confused. "Something's the matter with your head!" he said. "Are you feeling ill? Are you dizzy? It *is* a very hot day!"

"No, I'm not ill," said Cedric. "I'm sorry to say it's true: I *am* going to be an earl. Mr. Havisham was telling Dearest, and he's a lawyer. My grandfather sent him all the way from England to tell us."

Mr. Hobbs stared wildly at Cedric. "Who is your grandfather?" he asked.

Cedric took out a piece of paper from his pocket. "I couldn't remember it, so I wrote it down," he said. And he read slowly: "'John Arthur Molyneux Errol, Earl of Dorincourt.' He lives in a castle — in two or three castles, I think. Now I have to go live with him."

Cedric did not seem happy about his news.

"England is very far away, isn't it?" he asked.

"Across the Atlantic Ocean," said Mr. Hobbs.

"That's the worst of it," said Cedric. "I shall not see you again for a long time. I don't like to think of that, Mr. Hobbs."

"Even the best of friends must part," said Mr. Hobbs.

The two were quiet for some moments. Then they began to talk of what Cedric would do once he became an earl. Cedric said he would be a good one. He would not be a tyrant. If there was another war with America, he would try to stop it, he told Mr. Hobbs. He said a great many things that would have surprised Mr. Havisham. Mr. Havisham didn't know very many young boys, especially boys as smart and good-hearted as Cedric.

But there were many things that surprised Mr. Havisham. He had spent all of his life in

England, and he was not used to Americans. He didn't know much about the life that Captain Errol had made for himself in America. When Mr. Havisham met Mrs. Errol in her plain, tiny home, he was surprised to find that he liked her.

She was quite pretty, with a faint sad look on her young face. Mr. Havisham saw right away that she must have loved Captain Errol with all her heart. It was clear that she hadn't married him simply because he was an earl's son.

When he told Mrs. Errol that the old earl wanted Cedric to live with him in England, she grew pale.

"He'll be taken away from me?" she asked. "But he is such a happiness to me! He is all I have." Her voice trembled.

Mr. Havisham cleared his throat.

"I must tell you," he said, "that the Earl of Dorincourt is not very . . . friendly toward you. He does not like America or Americans. He was very angry about your marriage to his son, and he does not want to see you. His plan is for Lord Fauntleroy to live with him in Dorincourt Castle. The earl offers you a home at Court Lodge, which is not very far from the castle. He also offers you a good income. Lord Fauntleroy may visit you, but you may not visit him."

Mr. Havisham was embarrassed. He was afraid Mrs. Errol would begin to cry.

But she didn't cry. She went to the window and stood with her face turned away from him. Then she said, "Captain Errol was very fond of Dorincourt. It was a grief to him that he was parted from his home. He would wish—I know he would wish—for his son to go."

Then she came back to the table. She looked at Mr. Havisham gently.

"I know," she said, then started again. "I am *sure* the earl would not be so unkind as to try to teach Cedric not to love me. And I know—even if he tried—Cedric would still love me. As long as we may see each other, I will not suffer too much."

She cares so much more for her son than she does for herself, Mr. Havisham thought. *She doesn't realize how hard it will be for her.*

"Madam," he said, "I respect your decision. I assure you that every effort will be made so that Lord Fauntleroy will be happy."

When Cedric arrived back home, he went into the parlor to talk to Mr. Havisham. Mrs. Errol left them alone. Cedric wanted to know what exactly an earl was, since one day he would be one.

Mr. Havisham explained that an earl is a very important person in England.

"Like the president!" Cedric said.

"Not exactly," said Mr. Havisham. "An earl is often of very ancient lineage."

"What's that?" asked Cedric.

"Of very old family—very, very old."

"Ah," said Cedric, "I suppose it's that way with the apple-woman in the park. She is so old, it would surprise you how she can stand up. She's a hundred years old, I should think."

"I am afraid you did not quite understand me," Mr. Havisham explained. "When I said 'ancient lineage,' I didn't mean old age. I meant that the name of the family has been known in the world for a long time. The first Earl of Dorincourt was made an earl four hundred years ago."

"Well, well!" said Cedric. "That *was* a long time ago! What does an earl do?"

"A great many of them have helped to rule England. Some of them have been brave men and fought in great battles."

"I should like to do that," said Cedric. "My papa was a soldier, and he was a very brave man—as brave as George Washington. I'm glad that earls are brave. That's a good thing."

"There is another good thing about being an earl," said Mr. Havisham slowly. "Some earls have a lot of money."

"That *is* good," Cedric said innocently. "I wish I had a lot of money."

"Why?" asked Mr. Havisham.

"Well," explained Cedric, "there's the apple-woman. If I were very rich, I would buy her a tent and a little stove. And then—oh! I'd give her a shawl so her bones wouldn't feel so bad. Her bones are not like our bones. They hurt when she moves. If I were rich enough to help her, I guess her bones would be all right."

"And what else would you do if you were rich?" asked Mr. Havisham.

"Of course I'd buy Dearest all sorts of pretty things. And then Dick—"

"Who is Dick?" Mr. Havisham interrupted.

"Dick is one of the nicest shoe-shine boys you ever knew. He's about twelve years old, I think.

He works on the corner. Once, when I was very little, I was out with Dearest and she bought me a ball. The ball bounced into the street, where the carriages and horses were. I began to cry—I was very little. Then Dick stopped shining a man's shoes and ran in between the horses and caught the ball for me. Ever since, we stop to talk to him when we pass by."

"And what would you do for Dick?" asked Mr. Havisham, trying not to smile.

"I would help him buy out the shoe-shine business, of course. Dick has the worst partner— his name's Jake. Jake cheats. He makes Dick look bad. If I were rich, I would make Dick the boss."

"Is there anything you would get for yourself if you were rich?" asked Mr. Havisham.

"Lots of things!" Cedric said quickly. "But first I would give Mary some money for Bridget— that's her sister. Bridget has twelve children, and her husband, Michael, is out of work. And I think Mr. Hobbs would like a good watch."

Just then, Mrs. Errol came in.

"I'm sorry to have left you for so long," she said to Mr. Havisham. "But Mary's sister came to see me."

"This young gentleman," said Mr. Havisham, "has been telling me about some of his friends, and what he would do for them if he were rich."

"Bridget is one of his friends," said Mrs. Errol. "She is in great trouble now because her husband is very sick."

Cedric slipped off his big chair. "I think I'll go and see her," he said, and ran out of the room.

"Mrs. Errol," Mr. Havisham said, "the earl wanted me to let his lordship know that the change in his life would bring him money and the pleasures children enjoy. I was told to buy Cedric anything he wants, and to tell him that it is from his grandfather. If it would make Lord Fauntleroy happy to help this poor woman, the earl might be pleased."

"Oh, that was very kind of the earl. Cedric will be so glad!"

"If you will allow me," said Mr. Havisham, "I will give him five pounds for Bridget and her family."

"That's twenty-five dollars!" exclaimed Mrs. Errol. "They could buy medicine and warm clothing. It would mean so much to them."

Mrs. Errol left the room to find Cedric.

"Mr. Havisham has some news for you," she told him.

"News?" Cedric said. His little face looked quite anxious. He was sorry for Bridget.

Mrs. Errol brought Cedric back to the parlor.

"Ceddie," she said, "your grandpapa the earl is very, very kind. He wishes you to be happy and to make other people happy. He gave Mr. Havisham a great deal of money for you. You can give some to Bridget now—enough to pay her rent and buy Michael everything he needs. Isn't that fine, Ceddie? Isn't your grandfather good?" She kissed his cheek.

Cedric looked up in amazement. "Can I have it now?" he cried. "She is just leaving."

Mr. Havisham gave him the money, and Cedric flew out of the room.

"Bridget!" they heard him shout. "Bridget! Don't go! I have some money for you and Michael. My grandpapa gave it to me!"

"Master Ceddie!" cried Bridget. "This is so much money! Where is your mother?"

"I must go and explain it to her," Mrs. Errol said. So she, too, left the room, and Mr. Havisham was alone for a while.

He thought about the old Earl of Dorincourt, sitting in his giant, gloomy library at the castle. He was always ill with the gout, a disease that made his feet swell up. And he was always grumpy. There was never a more unpopular old nobleman than the Earl of Dorincourt, or a more selfish one. He had quite a lot of money, and he didn't like to share it.

Cedric was a cheery, handsome little boy who cared about all his many friends. He was so very generous.

Mr. Havisham thought of how rich Cedric would be one day. *It will make a great difference,* he said to himself.

CHAPTER 3

Leaving Home

༄

The week before they sailed for England, Cedric did many things, thanks to his grandfather. He helped the very old apple-woman of ancient lineage by giving her a stove and a shawl and some money. When he gave her the money, she gasped. She could hardly believe her great fortune.

Cedric also helped his friend Dick, the shoeshine boy. He went to the corner to tell him the news. He said that he had become a lord, and was in danger of being an earl if he lived long enough.

Dick jumped, and his cap fell off.

"I didn't think I would like it myself," Cedric said. "But I like it better now that I'm used to it. The one who is the earl now—he's my grand-father—is very kind. He sent me a lot of money, and I've brought some so you can buy the business from Jake."

Cedric tried to speak steadily, but his voice trembled a little. "Well, good-bye. And I hope business will be good. I'm sorry I'm going away. But I hope you'll write to me, because we were always good friends. And if you write, here's where you must send your letter." He gave Jake a slip of paper. "And my name isn't Cedric Errol anymore. It's Lord Fauntleroy and—and good-bye, Dick."

Dick blinked his eyes to keep from crying. He was so surprised, he didn't know what to say. "I wish you wasn't goin' away," was all he got out.

Then he blinked his eyes again. And when he opened them, Cedric was gone.

Cedric also made Mr. Hobbs promise to write him, and gave him a gold watch and chain.

Mr. Hobbs was depressed about his friend leaving. He felt funny about taking such an expensive gift. He laid the case on his stout knee and blew his nose several times.

"There's something written on it," said Cedric. "It says 'From his oldest friend, Lord Fauntleroy, to Mr. Hobbs. When this you see, remember me.' I don't want you to forget me."

Mr. Hobbs blew his nose very loudly again. "I won't forget you," he said. "And don't you forget me when you get among those British lords."

"I shouldn't forget you whoever I was among," said Cedric. "I hope you will come see me sometime. I'm sure my grandfather would be pleased. You—you wouldn't stay away just because he's an earl, would you?"

"I'd come to see you," replied Mr. Hobbs.

So it was agreed that if Mr. Hobbs received an invitation from the earl to come and spend some time at Dorincourt Castle, he would ignore how he felt about earls and pack his suitcase right away.

At last the day came for Cedric to leave for England. The trunks were taken to the ship, and the carriage waited at the door.

When Mrs. Errol came downstairs, her eyes were large and wet. Her mouth trembled.

Cedric put his arms around her. "We liked this little house, Dearest, didn't we?" he said. "And we will always like it, won't we?"

"Yes, darling," she answered in a low voice.

And then, before they knew it, they were on

the ship. There was noise and confusion everywhere. Carriages were parked all along the shore. Big trunks and cases were being bumped down and dragged about. Sailors were hurrying to and fro. Officers were giving orders. Ladies and gentlemen and children and nurses were coming on board.

Suddenly Cedric noticed someone coming toward him. It was a boy with something red in his hand. It was Dick!

"I've run all the way," Dick said, out of breath. "Business has been prime. I bought this for you out o' what I made yesterday. It's a handkerchief."

A bell rang and he leaped away before Cedric had time to speak.

"Good-bye!" Dick panted. "I hope you like it!"

A few seconds later, Cedric saw him struggle through the crowd and rush off the ship just in time. Dick stood on the shore and waved his cap as the ship started to pull away.

Cedric waved his new handkerchief back. It was made of bright red silk, with purple horse-shoes and horses' heads embroidered on it.

"Good-bye, Dick!" he shouted, hoping his friend could still hear him. "Thank you!"

CHAPTER 4

In England

⤳

When they were far out on the ocean, Cedric's mother told him that his home was not to be hers. Cedric's grief was so great that Mr. Havisham realized it was wise to make sure that the boy's mother lived nearby and saw him often. Cedric wouldn't be happy without her.

Mrs. Errol did her best to make sure her son wasn't afraid. "My house is not very far from the castle, Ceddie," she said every time he asked. "You can see me every day. You will have so many things to tell me. It's a beautiful place. Your papa told me about it. He loved it very much, and you will love it, too."

"I'd love it better if you were there," he said.

Mrs. Errol had decided not to tell him that it was his grandfather's idea to keep them apart. She told Mr. Havisham that she didn't want Cedric to learn the truth until he was older. "He wouldn't understand," she said. "It wouldn't make sense to him that anyone could hate me."

So all Cedric knew was that there was a strange reason he wasn't old enough to understand.

Soon the ship reached England, and a carriage drove Mr. Havisham, Cedric, and Mrs. Errol to Court Lodge, where Mrs. Errol would live. They reached the house at night, so it was too dark to see what it looked like.

Cedric saw only an open door. He could make out two servants standing in the doorway.

The servants looked with curiosity at both the boy and his mother. They had heard all sorts of rumors. They knew all about the boy's mean old grandfather, with his gout and his bad temper. They knew how angry the earl had been when his son had married this woman. They knew why Mrs. Errol had to live at the lodge, while her little boy lived at the castle.

But they didn't know what sort of little lord he would be.

Cedric pulled off his coat as if he was used to doing things for himself. Then he looked around the lodge. "Dearest," he said, "this is a very pretty house, isn't it? I'm glad you are going to live here. It's quite large."

It *was* a large house, compared to the one in New York, but Mrs. Errol looked a little pale and upset. She pulled Mr. Havisham aside. "Could he stay with me tonight?" she asked in a low voice.

"Of course," Mr. Havisham answered quietly. "I will go tell the earl that we have arrived."

"Having to live apart from my little boy will be so very difficult," Mrs. Errol said sadly. "Will you tell the earl that I would rather not have the money?"

"You cannot mean that!" Mr. Havisham exclaimed. He pulled her away so Cedric wouldn't hear.

"I do mean it," she said. "I must accept the house, and I thank him for it. It makes it possible for me to be near my child. But I have a little money of my own—enough to live simply—and I would rather not take his."

"He will be very angry," Mr. Havisham said. "He won't understand."

"I think he will," she said. "Why should I accept gifts from the man who hates me so much that he takes away my own child?"

"I'll deliver your message," Mr. Havisham replied.

Mr. Havisham went to the castle, where he found the old earl sitting by the fire in his easy chair. His bad foot was up on his footstool.

"Well," the earl said, "what's the news?"

"Lord Fauntleroy and his mother are at Court Lodge," replied Mr. Havisham. "They are in excellent health."

The earl made a gruff sound. "What else?" he asked. "I don't care about the mother. What sort of lad is he?"

"It is rather difficult to judge," Mr. Havisham said. "He is only seven."

"A fool, is he?" the earl exclaimed. "Clumsy? His American blood shows, does it?"

"I don't know much about children, but I thought he was a rather fine lad."

"Well enough to look at?" demanded the earl.

A very slight smile touched Mr. Havisham's

lips. "Rather a handsome boy, I think, as boys go. But I dare say you will find him somewhat different from most English children."

"I haven't a doubt," snarled the earl. "Rude little beggars, those American children."

"Not rude," said Mr. Havisham. "He has lived more with older people than with children."

"Bad manners!" shouted the earl.

Mr. Havisham didn't argue. When the earl was upset, it was always better to leave him alone. So there was silence for several moments.

Then Mr. Havisham said, "I have a message from Mrs. Errol."

"I don't want any of her messages!" growled the earl. "The less I hear of her, the better."

"This is rather important. She does not want the money you planned to give her."

The earl jumped. "She wants to make me see her! She thinks I shall admire her spirit. I don't admire it! I won't have her living like a beggar at my gates! She is the boy's mother! She has a position to keep up! She shall have the money, whether she likes it or not!"

"She won't spend it," said Mr. Havisham.

"I don't care! It will be sent to her anyway. She wants to give the boy a bad opinion of me. She has poisoned his mind against me!"

"She hasn't," said Mr. Havisham. "In fact, she would prefer that you not tell him why you keep him away from her. He is very fond of her. She thinks that if he knows the truth, he may not like you."

The earl sank back in his chair. His fierce old eyes gleamed. "Come now!" he said. "You don't mean the mother hasn't told him?"

"Not a word, my lord. The boy is ready to believe that you are the most loving of grandparents. And from what he learned of you in New York, he thinks you are very generous."

"He does, eh?" said the earl.

"I give you my word of honor. But if you will pardon my saying so, I think it would be best if you do not say a bad word about his mother."

"Pooh, pooh!" said the earl. "He's only seven years old!"

"Yes, and he has spent those seven years at his mother's side," said Mr. Havisham. "She has all his love."

The earl did not respond. Mr. Havisham waited a long time until the earl was asleep, and he could take his leave.

CHAPTER 5

At the Castle

⌒

"It's the most beautiful place I've ever seen!" Cedric said the next morning as the carriage approached Dorincourt Castle. "It reminds me of a king's palace I saw in a picture book once."

Dorincourt Castle was one of the grandest in all of England. It rose up stately and gray. The windows dazzled in the sun. It had turrets and battlements and towers. All around it were grand terraces and beds of brilliantly colored flowers.

Cedric saw the great entrance door thrown open. Dozens of servants were waiting before it in two lines. The tallest footman took him to the library. He opened the door and announced, "Lord Fauntleroy, my lord."

Cedric entered the room. It was very large and fancy. But the furniture was so dark and the curtains so heavy that the room looked gloomy. For a moment, Cedric thought that nobody was there, but then he saw a fire burning. Someone was sitting in the easy chair before the fireplace— someone who didn't turn to look at him.

A large dog was lying on the floor next to the easy chair. When he saw Cedric, he rose slowly and marched toward him.

At that, the person in the chair spoke. "Dougal," he called to the dog, "come back here."

But Cedric was not afraid of the giant dog. He put his hand on the dog's huge collar in the most natural way in the world. Then they walked forward together, Dougal sniffing him as they went.

Finally the earl looked up, and Cedric saw a large old man with shaggy white hair and eyebrows. He had a nose like an eagle's beak and deep, fierce eyes.

The earl saw a graceful boy in a black velvet suit, with curly blond hair and a handsome face. His eyes met the earl's without any fear.

There was a glow of pride in the fiery old earl's heart. He could see what a strong, beautiful boy his grandson was. It pleased him that the boy didn't seem afraid—not of the dog, and not of him.

"You must be the earl," Cedric said. "I'm your grandson, you know. I'm Lord Fauntleroy."

He held out his hand. "I hope you are very well," he continued. "I'm glad to see you."

The earl shook hands with him. He was so surprised at how charming the boy was that he didn't know what to say.

"I wondered what you would look like,"

Cedric said. "I wondered if you would look like my father."

"Do I?" asked the earl.

"Well," Cedric said, "I was just three when he died. I may not remember exactly how he looked, but I don't think you do."

"You are disappointed, I suppose?" suggested his grandfather.

"Oh, no!" said Cedric. "Of course you would like anyone to look like your father, but of course you would enjoy the way your grandfather looks, too. He *is* your grandfather."

The earl leaned back in his chair and stared.

"Any boy would love his grandfather," continued Cedric. "Especially one who has been so kind."

"I have been kind to you, have I?"

"Oh, yes," said Cedric. "Thank you for Bridget and the apple-woman and Dick!"

"Bridget!" exclaimed the earl. "Dick! The apple-woman!"

"The ones you gave me the money for," Cedric explained.

"Ha!" said the earl. "That's it! The money you were to spend as you liked. What did you buy?"

Cedric explained how he had helped all of his friends. "It's all thanks to you," he said.

As Cedric talked, the earl became more and more shocked. He never thought he would like his grandson. He had sent away for the boy out of pride. Now it was almost too good to be true that this was the little boy he had dreaded meeting. The child of the woman he so disliked had so much beauty and grace!

Relaxing in his chair, the earl let his grandson talk. The boy told him all about Mr. Hobbs. Then the conversation turned to the Fourth of July and the American Revolution. Cedric was getting excited, but suddenly he stopped talking.

"What's the matter?" demanded his grand-father. "Why don't you go on?"

Cedric flushed. "I was only thinking that you might not like what I was saying. I forgot that you are an Englishman."

"You forgot *you* are an Englishman, you mean."

"I'm an American," Cedric said.

"You *are* an Englishman," said the earl grimly. "Your father was an Englishman."

Seeing his grandson act so serious—and about being an American, of all things—amused the earl. But the boy did not seem amused.

"I was born in America," he protested. "You have to be American if you were born in America."

The earl gave a half-laugh. It was short, but it was a laugh.

He hated America and Americans, but such a good American might make a rather good Englishman when he grew to be a man.

Then dinner was announced. A footman arrived to help the earl into the dining room.

Cedric went to his grandfather and looked down at his gouty foot.

"Would you like me to help you?" he asked politely. "You could lean on me. Once, when a potato barrel rolled over Mr. Hobbs's foot, he leaned on me."

The earl gazed down at Cedric. "Well," he said, "you may try."

Cedric gave the earl his stick and helped him to stand. Usually the footman did this, and was yelled at when the earl's foot throbbed from the gout. But tonight the earl didn't yell, even though his foot did hurt. He decided to try an experiment. He got up slowly and put his hand on his grandson's small shoulder. Then he leaned down.

Cedric took a careful step forward. "Just lean on me," he said. "I'll walk slowly."

It was part of the earl's experiment to let his grandson feel how heavy he was. He wanted to see what the boy would do.

Cedric's face grew quite hot, and his heart beat fast, but he kept walking. It wasn't very far to the dining room, though it seemed a long way to Cedric. The hand on his shoulder grew heavier with each step, and the boy's face became hotter. But he never once thought of giving up.

At last they reached the chair. The earl took his hand from Cedric's shoulder and sat down.

The old man was so fond of his dinner, he dined in a formal style even when he was alone. The room was very grand, with many servants and bright lights and glittering silver and glass. The earl sat at the head of the table, and Cedric sat at the foot.

The earl kept the boy talking throughout dinner. He never imagined that he could be entertained by listening to a child talk, but the boy puzzled and amused him.

He kept thinking of how he had let the boy feel his full weight when he helped him into the dining room. He'd wanted to test his grandson's courage. It pleased him to know that the boy did not give up.

"You must be very proud of your house," Cedric said. "I've never seen anything so beautiful. Of course, I am only seven and I haven't seen much. It's a very big house for just two people to live in, isn't it?"

"It is quite large enough for two," answered the earl. "Do you find it too large?"

Cedric hesitated a moment.

"I was only thinking," he said, "that if two people lived in it who were not very good companions, they might feel lonely sometimes."

"Do you think I shall make a good companion?" asked the earl.

"Yes," said Cedric. "I think you will. Mr. Hobbs and I were great friends. He was the best friend I had, except for Dearest."

"Who is Dearest?"

"She is my mother," Cedric said in a quiet voice.

He could not help thinking about her. And the more he thought of her, the less he wanted to talk. By the time dinner had ended and they went back to the library, the earl saw that there was a faint shadow on the boy's face.

The earl watched Cedric as he sat on a rug near Dougal. For a few minutes, he stroked the dog's ears in silence and looked at the fire. Once or twice the boy sighed.

"Cedric," the earl said at last, "what are you thinking of?"

Cedric looked up and tried to smile.

"I was thinking about Dearest. And—and I'd better get up and walk around the room. It helps me think."

He stood up and put his hands in his small pockets. Then he began to pace to and fro.

Dougal followed. Cedric removed a hand from his pocket and petted the dog's head.

"He's a very nice dog," he said. "He's my friend. He knows how I feel."

"Come here," the earl said. "How do you feel?"

"I've never been so far away from home before," the boy said, a troubled look in his brown eyes. "It makes a person feel strange when he has to stay all night in a new place. But Dearest is not very far away from here. She told me to remember that. And—and I can look at the picture she gave me."

He took out a small velvet-covered case from his pocket.

"This is it," he said. "You see, you press this spring and it opens. And she is in there!" The case opened, and he looked up with a smile.

The earl did not wish to see the picture. But

he looked at it anyway and saw a pretty young face — a face a lot like the boy's.

"I suppose you are very fond of her," he said.

"Yes," said Cedric. "It's true. My father left Dearest to me to take care of."

The earl didn't speak again. He leaned back in his chair and watched the boy. A great many strange new thoughts passed through the old nobleman's mind. There was a long silence.

Half an hour later, Mr. Havisham arrived. The great room was very still when he entered. The earl was still leaning back in his chair. He moved as Mr. Havisham approached and, without thinking, held up a hand to warn him. Dougal was asleep. And close beside the great dog, also sleeping, lay little Lord Fauntleroy.

CHAPTER 6

The Earl's Grandson

⌒

Cedric's first morning in the castle was a curious one. As he was waking up, he heard two women talking. Neither one was Dearest. One woman was telling the other to be careful not to say a word, but about what? He opened his eyes.

"Good morning, my lord," said a gentle voice. "Did you sleep well?"

Cedric said he had. But he didn't say how much he had missed Dearest, or how he wondered how she was doing this morning, waking up in the lodge by herself.

One of the women left to do the housekeeping, but the other woman stayed. Her name was Dawson. She was there to take care of him, she explained. "Will you get up and let me dress you, and have your breakfast in the nursery?"

"I learned how to dress myself years ago," Cedric said politely. "But thank you for offering. Dearest taught me. I can do it myself, except sometimes I need a little help with the buttons."

At last he was dressed and having his breakfast in the nursery. He asked Dawson many questions about her life. He found out that Dawson's husband had been a soldier and had died in battle. Her son was a sailor and had seen practically the whole world. Dawson had taken care of little children all her life. Soon enough, they were great friends.

Cedric could see that there was another room next to the nursery, and another one next to that. There were so many rooms in this giant house, he could hardly imagine counting them all.

"I'm so little to live in such a big castle, don't you think?" he asked Dawson.

"Oh, you'll like it here soon enough," Dawson told him. "It only feels strange at first."

"What feels the strangest is being apart from Dearest," Cedric said. "I miss her. I always had my breakfast with her. I put the sugar and cream in her tea, and I handed her the toast."

"But you can see her every day," Dawson assured him. "And you will have so much to tell her once you see the dogs and the horses . . . and you haven't even seen what's in the next room."

Cedric couldn't help but be curious. "What's in there?" he asked.

"You must finish your breakfast first, and then I will show you," Dawson teased.

Cedric ate quickly. When he was at last finished, Dawson took him to the next room. The room was filled with the most spectacular toys a boy could imagine. Cedric had seen such toys—but only in store windows in New York. He had never had any of his own to play with.

"Whose toys are these?" Cedric asked. He wondered if he might be able to play with some of them.

Dawson laughed. "Don't you know?" she said. "They're all yours!"

"But who gave them to me? Was it my grandfather? Oh, it was, wasn't it? It had to be!"

"Yes, it was," Dawson said. "And if you're a good boy, this won't be all he'll give you. He'll give you anything you want."

Cedric could scarcely imagine such a thing. The room full of toys was more than enough. He couldn't wait to tell Dearest all about them.

"Did you ever know anyone who had such a kind grandfather?" he asked Dawson as he found a game board to play with.

Dawson made a strange face. It seemed like she wanted to say something, but she didn't.

The truth was, Dawson didn't have a high opinion of the earl. She'd only been working in his house for a short time and already she'd heard the stories about how mean he was to the servants and the people who lived on his lands. From what Dawson had heard, he was not a kind man at all.

But what she and Cedric didn't know was that the earl had not given his grandson this room full of toys to be kind. He wanted the shelves and closets stocked full of amusements. He wanted the boy to have everything he could hope for—every possible distraction.

"Give him what will amuse him," the earl had said, "and he will forget his mother soon enough." That was the plan.

And Cedric *was* kept amused all morning by his toys and games. Later in the afternoon, when his grandfather at last sent for him, Cedric came running down the stairs. He burst into the room with his eyes sparkling and his cheeks flushed.

"Thank you so much!" he said. "For the toys and the games and for everything! Thank you!"

The earl calmly sat back in his chair. "I see you like them," he said, feeling satisfied.

"Oh, I do," Cedric said. "I truly do. And there's one game—it's like baseball, only you play it on a board with black and white pegs. Will play with me? I'll show you how."

The earl didn't play games. "I'm afraid I don't know baseball. It's an American game, isn't it?"

"I can show you!" Cedric said. "You might like it. It might help you forget about your foot. Is it hurting much today?"

"More than I'd like it to," the earl said. "Go and get the game."

Cedric raced upstairs and returned with the game board. Soon they were playing the game together, and the earl was surprised to find that he was actually enjoying it. His grandson had an odd effect on him.

Suddenly they were interrupted by a visitor, Reverend Mordaunt of the local church. It was his duty to pay visits to the earl, often to ask for help when someone on the earl's lands was in trouble.

The earl hated to be bothered by other people's troubles. If he was in a nasty mood—if his gout was worse than usual—he would yell and send Reverend Mordaunt off with nothing. If he was in a less nasty mood—if his foot was feeling all right that day—he might help with a little money. It all depended on how he felt, and Reverend Mordaunt never knew what to expect.

That day the reverend was shocked by what he found. When he entered the room, the delightful ring of childish laughter greeted him. There was the earl in his usual chair, and there beside him was a beautiful little boy leaning his arm on the earl's healthy knee. They were playing a game as if they were good friends.

Reverend Mordaunt knew all about the earl's grandson—everyone in town had heard the stories. But he certainly didn't expect that the earl would be playing with the boy, and seeming to enjoy his company. It was a sight.

When the earl saw Reverend Mordaunt in the doorway, his face turned harsh. In his usual gruff voice he said, "Good day, Mordaunt. What is it you want now?"

Reverend Mordaunt took a moment to be properly introduced to the little boy, the new Lord Fauntleroy.

"I am glad to meet you, sir," said Cedric, reaching out to shake Reverend Mordaunt's hand.

Reverend Mordaunt couldn't help but smile. He liked the boy right away, like most people did. He could tell that the boy had a good heart.

"Take a chair, Mordaunt," the earl said. "Well, who is in trouble now?"

"It's Higgins," Mordaunt explained. "Higgins of Edge Farm. He has had some terrible bad luck. He was ill himself, and his children had scarlet fever, and now his wife is ill. Higgins is having trouble making his rent now. His landlord is Newick, and I know Newick works for you, managing all the lands. Newick has told Higgins that he and his family will be out on the street if he doesn't pay. Higgins begged me to see you about it. He needs money for medicine and food. He thinks if you gave him some time to catch up on the rent . . ."

"They all want that," the earl snapped. He had a stormy look on his face.

Cedric, however, was very interested in Higgins. He wondered how many children there were. He wondered if the scarlet fever had hurt them very much. He didn't want Higgins and his family to be out on the street.

He turned to his grandfather. "Oh, how will you help him?" he asked innocently.

The earl gazed at him in silence. "Help him?" he repeated.

"Yes," Cedric answered. Clearly it hadn't occurred to him that his grandfather wouldn't help.

"And how would *you* help?" the earl asked Cedric. "If you were able to."

Reverend Mordaunt held his breath. He realized what a great deal of power this boy might
have, to do with as he pleased. If the young boy
wasn't good, it might be the worst thing that
could happen. For everyone.

"If I was very rich," Cedric began, "and not
just a little boy, I would talk to Newick and tell
him to let Higgins stay, of course. And I would
give Higgins the things he needs for his children.
But then, I am only a boy."

Suddenly his face brightened as an idea came
to him. "But you," he said, looking up at his
grandfather, "*you* can do anything, can't you?"

"Humph!" said the earl. "Is that so?" But he
didn't seem angry.

"Yes," said Cedric. "Are you going to write
Newick a letter now, and ask him to let Higgins
stay?"

The earl paused for a moment. Then he asked,
"Can you write?"

"Yes," Cedric said. "But not very well."

"Then you write it," his grandfather said.

"Me!"

"Yes, you. Bring the pen and ink and a sheet of paper from my desk."

Cedric hurried to get the supplies. Reverend Mordaunt watched in wonder as the earl spoke, and the little boy carefully copied his words onto the paper in his childish handwriting, spelling errors and all. The earl seemed amused by the whole process, even when Cedric insisted on copying the letter over and over again, asking about the words he didn't know how to spell, so there wouldn't be as many mistakes.

At last, the letter was ready and Cedric handed it to Reverend Mordaunt. The reverend left Dorincourt Castle feeling hopeful. He had never felt such a thing after being there. And it was all thanks to the little boy.

After Reverend Mordaunt was gone, Cedric

went back to his grandfather's side. "May I see Dearest now?" he asked.

"Now?" the earl said. "You haven't even seen the stables yet."

"I can see them tomorrow. I'm sure Dearest is waiting for me."

"But I didn't tell you what is in the stables. It's a pony."

"A pony!" Cedric exclaimed. "Whose pony?"

"Yours," replied the earl.

"Mine!" cried the boy. "Mine? Like all the toys upstairs?"

"Yes," the earl said, feeling very satisfied. "Let us go see your pony now."

Cedric drew a long breath. "I want to see it," he said. "I want to see it very much. But I'm afraid there isn't time. Dearest is waiting."

"Must you go see your mother this afternoon?" the earl asked.

"Oh, yes," Cedric said. "She has been thinking

of me all day, and I have been thinking of her. Now I can't wait to tell her all about the pony."

"So you've been thinking of her, have you?" the earl said. "Fine. Let's go."

They rode together to the lodge in a carriage. Cedric asked many questions about the pony. He wanted to know what color it was, how big it was, what it liked to eat, and if it had a name.

As they approached the lodge, Cedric turned to his grandfather and exclaimed, "You make so many people so happy! Do you know, I've counted on my fingers and you've been kind to twenty-seven people. Twenty-seven! That's a lot!"

"And I was the person who was kind to them, was I?" said the earl.

"Of course," said Cedric.

They had reached the lodge. Cedric leaped out of the carriage and then turned back, confused. The earl wasn't getting out.

"Aren't you coming in to see Dearest?" Cedric asked.

"No," his grandfather replied.

"Not—not see Dearest?" Cedric said, astonished. "She will be so disappointed."

I doubt that, the earl thought to himself.

He told his footman to close the carriage door and watched as Cedric ran up the path toward the house. The earl could see the house through the trees. The door was wide open.

In the doorway stood a slender figure—a pretty young woman dressed all in black. The little boy ran to his mother, then leaped into her arms and covered her face with kisses.

CHAPTER 7

At Church

Sunday morning, the earl decided that he and his grandson would attend church. He rarely went, but the family pew was always left empty for him in case he did. This Sunday he wanted to go because he would have Cedric at his side. People from the village would be there, so he'd have the chance to show the boy off.

Almost the whole town showed up that Sunday. They waited outside the church to catch sight of the earl and his grandson. Everyone had heard the story of the little Lord Fauntleroy, and how he had helped Higgins.

They also knew about the little lord's poor mother, who was forced to live apart from him, and who the earl hated for no reason. No one could stop talking about it.

Everyone stared as Mrs. Errol approached the church. One old woman curtsied. Then another woman curtsied. A man took off his hat and bowed. Mrs. Errol didn't understand at first. Then she realized—they knew she was Lord Fauntleroy's mother. She flushed shyly and bowed, too. "Thank you," she said.

As she reached the church, a carriage drew up, and a boy dressed in black velvet jumped out. The crowd looked at him curiously.

"He looks just like the captain!" said a woman who remembered his father.

The little boy was waiting patiently beside the

carriage to help his grandfather. The old earl stepped out and leaned on his grandson, who led him toward the church.

Everyone in the crowd bowed and curtsied as the earl and his grandson walked past.

"Look how glad the people are to see you!" Cedric said.

"Take off your cap, Cedric," said the earl. "They are bowing to you."

"To me!" cried Cedric. He whipped off his cap, and his bright blond curls tumbled out. He turned, puzzled, and bowed to everyone.

Inside the church, Cedric and the earl sat in their cushioned and curtained pew. It was separate from the others, better and more private. Once Cedric was seated, he saw something that made him very happy. There, across the church, was his pretty mother, smiling at him. During the service, he listened and stood to sing the hymns. And all the while she was there, just across the room where he could see her.

Mrs. Errol couldn't help but watch him, too. As did the earl. He sat behind his curtain, eyeing his grandson as he sang. The little boy's voice was like a bird's. The earl liked the sound of it more than he thought he would.

The earl also stole a glance or two over the people's heads. There was his son's wife, sitting alone. He saw her pretty face. He saw that her eyes were almost exactly like her little boy's— the same warm, deep color brown.

As the earl and Cedric left the church, they came upon a man who had been waiting for them. He held his hat in his hand and took a step forward.

"Well, Higgins," said the earl.

"Oh!" Cedric said. "Mr. Higgins?"

"Yes," answered the earl. "And I suppose he has come to get a look at his new landlord."

"Yes, my lord," said Higgins. His sunburned face reddened. "I wanted to say a word of thanks. If I might be allowed."

The earl didn't respond, so Higgins turned to Cedric.

"I have a great deal to thank your lordship for——" he began.

"I only wrote the letter," said Cedric. "It was my grandfather who did it. But you know how he is, always being good to everybody. Is Mrs. Higgins feeling any better?"

Higgins wasn't sure what to say. The earl was

never good to anybody. "I—well, yes, your lordship," he stammered. "She is doing better."

"I'm glad to hear that," said Cedric. "My grandfather was very sorry about your children having scarlet fever, and so was I."

Higgins was in a panic. He couldn't look the earl in the eye—not when he knew the truth. The earl hated children. Everybody knew that. It was said that when his own sons were boys, he didn't even like *them*. Higgins doubted very much that the Earl of Dorincourt cared whether or not his children had been sick with scarlet fever.

"You see, Higgins," the earl broke in with a grim smile, "you people have been wrong about me. Lord Fauntleroy understands me. When you want honest information about me, just ask him. Now get into the carriage, Cedric."

Cedric jumped in, and the carriage rolled away. As it turned the corner, the earl had a grim smile on his face. He was very pleased.

CHAPTER 8

Learning to Ride

∽

The Earl of Dorincourt had the chance to wear his grim smile many times as the days passed. The more time he spent with Cedric, the more often he smiled. Sometimes his smile didn't even seem that grim.

On the morning Cedric learned to ride his pony, the earl was so pleased, he almost forgot about his gout. Wilkins, the groom, had brought out the fine brown pony, and the earl had found a seat near his window so he could watch. This was Cedric's very first riding lesson. The earl wondered if the boy would be scared and—like most children—start to cry.

But Cedric did no such thing. He had never been on a pony before, and he was very excited. The groom had him sit in the saddle by himself. Then he slowly led the pony in front of the window so the earl could see.

After a few minutes, Cedric spoke up to his grandfather. "Can't I go by myself?" he asked. "And can't I go faster? I want to trot and canter."

"Do you think you could?" asked the earl.

"I would like to try," said Cedric.

"Then let him trot," the earl told Wilkins.

The next few minutes were exciting. Cedric learned that trotting on the pony wasn't as easy as it looked. The faster the pony trotted, the harder it was.

"It j-jolts a g-goo-good deal—does-doesn't it?" he said.

The earl watched him bounce past. Cedric's

cheeks grew bright red. He looked like he was out of breath. But he held on, and he kept going. Then Cedric and Wilkins rode off into the trees. When they came back, the boy's cheeks were even redder. And his hat was missing.

"What happened to your hat?" called the earl.

Wilkins answered for him. "It fell off, your lordship. He wouldn't let me stop to pick it up."

"Ready to get off?" the earl asked the boy.

"It jolts you more than you think it will," admitted Cedric. "And it tires you a little, too. But I don't want to get off. I want to learn how to trot and canter faster. As soon as I catch my breath, I want to go back for the hat."

The boy was brave and determined, and the earl was impressed. He watched as Cedric and Wilkins trotted back into the trees. This time when they returned, they were riding much faster. And Wilkins had the lost hat.

Cedric's hair was flying in the wind. "There,"

he said as he came to a stop under his grandfather's window. He was out of breath. "I cantered! I stayed on!"

Cedric, Wilkins, and the pony were good friends after that. Almost every day they rode out together around the town. The children in the cottages would run out to wave to little Lord Fauntleroy. Cedric always shouted good morning and waved back.

Once, Cedric insisted on stopping at the village school. He noticed a boy who had hurt his leg, and he wanted the boy to ride home on his pony instead of having to walk.

When they reached the boy's cottage, his mother came out to greet Cedric. Cedric whipped off his cap and waved. "I've brought your son home, ma'am," he said. "His leg was hurting him. I don't think that stick is enough for him to lean on. I'm going to ask my grandfather to buy a pair of crutches for him."

When the earl heard about this, he wasn't angry. He was amused.

A few days later, he even took Cedric to the boy's house in his carriage. Cedric leaped out to deliver the crutches, as promised. When the boy's mother answered the door, he said, "My grandfather's compliments. If you please, these are for your boy. We hope he will get better."

Back in the carriage, he told the earl what he had said. "I said they were your compliments," he explained. "You didn't tell me to say that, but I thought you forgot. That was the right thing to say, wasn't it?"

The earl laughed, but he didn't say that it wasn't.

Cedric also saw Dearest every day. Mostly, he was happy. But there was one thing that puzzled him. He thought about it a lot—even though he didn't talk about it to the earl or to Dearest.

He thought it was strange that Dearest and his

grandfather never seemed to meet. When the carriage stopped at Court Lodge, the earl never got out to greet her. On the rare Sundays when the earl went to church, Cedric always ended up speaking with his mother alone.

And yet, fruit and flowers were sent to the lodge from the castle every day. And soon after the first Sunday, when Dearest had walked to church, the earl gave her a present. It was a large carriage with two horses. Cedric found it at her door one day when he was going to visit her.

"That is a present from you to your mother," the earl snapped. "She cannot go walking around the country. She needs a carriage. It is a present from *you*."

Fauntleroy was delighted. He ran to tell her. "Dearest! The carriage is yours! Can you believe it? He says it is a present from me!"

Cedric was so happy, his mother didn't know what to say. She didn't want to accept money or presents from the earl, but she knew that her son would not understand why.

Cedric often told Dearest stories about how good and noble and generous his grandfather was. His stories were so innocent that sometimes they made her laugh a little. She would pull him to her side and kiss him, feeling happy that he could see only the good in the old man.

Cedric also wrote to his friend, Mr. Hobbs. He showed the earl the letter before sending it, to make sure there were no spelling mistakes.

The letter told Mr. Hobbs what a great earl his grandfather was. He wasn't a tyrant, Cedric assured his old friend. The letter went on to describe the many things that the earl had done for his people and for Cedric. Cedric wrote that he wished his mother could live with him at the castle, but that he was very happy, when he didn't miss her too much.

When the earl finished reading this letter, he studied Cedric carefully. "Do you miss your mother that much?" he asked.

"I miss her all the time," the boy said. "*You* don't miss her, do you?"

"I don't know her," the earl snapped.

"I think that's odd," Cedric said. "Don't you? It makes me wonder. I know she said not to ask questions, but it does make me wonder. When I miss her very much, I look out my bedroom window at night and I can see the light in her window. It's very far away, through the trees, but it's there. She puts it on as soon as it's dark. I know what it says."

"What does it say?" the earl asked.

"It says: 'Good night. I am thinking of you.' So you see, I am always thinking of her, and she is always thinking of me."

"I have no doubt," the earl said.

CHAPTER 9

The Poor Cottages

Pride gave the Earl of Dorincourt a new interest in life. He was proud of his grandson's beauty and bravery. And since Cedric was his heir, it made him look good. The whole world had known of his disappointment with his own sons. Now he wanted to show Cedric off to the world. The new Lord Fauntleroy could disappoint no one.

Sometimes, in secret, the earl thought back to his life before Cedric had come into it. He wished he had been a better person. There were some things about the earl that Cedric's pure heart would shrink from, if he knew the truth.

For years the earl had been called the "Wicked Earl of Dorincourt." It made him nervous to think that someone might tell Cedric about this. He never wanted the boy to find out.

The earl also found that he liked spending time with the boy. Days would go by, and he would forget about his gout. Even the doctor said his health was better than ever expected.

One morning, Cedric came by on his pony. He looked up at the window where his grandfather often sat to watch. "I wish you were going with me," he called. "I don't like to leave you all alone in the big castle. It must be so lonely."

At that, the earl surprised everyone. He went to the stables and insisted that the groom prepare his horse. Soon enough, Lord Fauntleroy was riding his pony with a new companion, his grandfather. It was quite a sight. There was the tall, powerful, gray horse carrying the tall, gray old man. And beside it was the little brown pony that carried the little blond boy.

The two chatted as they went out riding along the green lanes and the pretty country roads. Cedric talked about a great many things—especially his mother. Gradually, the old man learned a lot about "Dearest" and her life.

It didn't displease him to learn that she was quite busy around town. Whenever anybody needed help, she was there. When there was sickness or sorrow or poverty in any house, she went to visit. Some people even visited her at Court Lodge to learn how to sew.

It also didn't displease the earl to find that his son's wife was so pretty. She looked as much like a lady as if she had been a duchess. He liked that she was popular and beloved by the poor. And yet, he sometimes felt jealous when Cedric spoke about her. The boy loved her more than he loved anyone else, and the earl wished that he was the one the boy loved most.

One morning as Cedric and the earl were out riding their horses, they came to a high hill where much of the earl's lands could be seen. It was beautiful and spread out in every direction.

"Do you know that all this land belongs to me?" the earl asked Cedric.

"Does it?" the boy asked. "It's so much land to belong to one person! And it's so pretty!"

"Someday it will all belong to you—this and a great deal more!"

"To me!" exclaimed Cedric, shocked. "When?"

"When I am dead," said his grandfather.

"Then I don't want it," said the boy. "I want you to live always."

"That's kind," the earl said. "Even so, one day all this land will be yours. One day, you will be the Earl of Dorincourt."

Cedric sat very still in his saddle. He looked out over the green hills and the farms and the cottages and the roads and the villages all around him. He looked over the trees at the turrets of the giant castle. Then he sighed.

"What's the matter?" asked the earl.

"I am only thinking of what Dearest said to me," Cedric replied. "She said that it is not easy to be very rich. If one always has so many things, one might sometimes forget that other people don't have those things. Someone who is very rich should always be careful to remember.

"I was telling her how kind you are, and she said that was good. She said that an earl has a lot of power. He can't think only of himself. He must think of all the people who live on his lands, and be there to help them if they need help.

"I was just looking out at all those houses. There are so many. And I was thinking that when I am an earl, I will have to find out about all the people who live in them. How do you find out about them?"

The earl's knowledge of the people who lived on his lands was very small. He knew only who paid the rent on time and who didn't.

"Newick—the man who manages all my lands—he finds out for me," the earl said. "Let's go home now. And when you are an earl, see to it that you are a better one than I have been!"

Cedric said he didn't think that would be possible, but he would do his best.

The earl was quiet on the way back to the castle.

About a week later, Cedric came into the library seeming upset. He looked into the fire for a long while. Clearly, he had something on his mind.

Finally, he looked away from the fire and spoke. "Does Newick know all about all the people?" he asked the earl.

"It is his job to know," the earl answered. "So he's not doing his job, then?" He didn't trust Newick completely. He didn't trust anyone.

The earl liked it when Cedric showed an interest in the tenants. He found it amusing how serious the boy became when he asked about them.

"There is a place," Cedric said, looking up with wide, scared eyes. "It is at the other end of the village. Dearest has seen it. The houses are close together and are almost falling down. You can hardly breathe. And the people are so poor, and everything is so dreadful! Often they have fever! It is worse than with Michael and Bridget! The rain comes in through the roof! Dearest went to see a poor woman who lives there, and wouldn't let me near her until she had changed all her clothes. She cried when she told me about it."

Tears came to Cedric's eyes.

"I told her that you didn't know," he said. "I told her I would tell you." He leaned against the earl's chair and put his hand on his grandfather's knee. "You can make it all right," he said. "Just as you made it all right for Higgins. I told her you would. I told her that Newick must have forgotten to tell you."

The earl looked down at the hand on his knee. Newick had not forgotten to tell him. In fact, Newick had talked to him more than once about the terrible problems at the end of the village of Erlesboro, in a place called Earl's Court. The old man knew all about the broken, leaky cottages and the sickness and the very poor people.

Reverend Mordaunt had even asked for the earl's help. But he had asked at a very bad time— when the gout was especially awful—and the earl had yelled at the reverend. He had said that the sooner the people of Earl's Court died and were buried, the sooner the place could be torn down.

And yet, as he looked at the small hand on his

knee, he felt ashamed. He was ashamed of Earl's Court. And he was ashamed of himself.

He put his hand on his grandson's hand. "What!" he said. "Do you want me to build them all new cottages to live in?"

"Yes!" Cedric said, now getting very excited. "The bad ones should be torn down, and we should build new ones! Let's start tomorrow!" His face was glowing. His eyes were shining like stars.

The earl rose from his chair. "Let's go take a walk," he said, "and we can talk it over."

CHAPTER 10

Extraordinary News

⌒

The truth was that Mrs. Errol had found many sad things in the village of Erlesboro. The people were poor and sick and feeling hopeless. When Mrs. Errol had first visited, it made her shudder. It was crowded and dirty and sad. As she watched the sick children running around with ragged clothes on their backs, she thought of her own son, spending his days in a splendid castle, living like a prince. And it gave her a bold idea.

Cedric had the good fortune of being the earl's favorite companion. The earl wanted to please the boy however he could. If there was something that Cedric wanted, the earl would not refuse him.

Mrs. Errol knew she could trust her son's kind, innocent heart. So she told him the story of Earl's Court. She told him everything. She felt sure that he would mention it to his grandfather.

The earl heard Cedric's story, but didn't know what to say at first. He knew he wasn't a good person. But he loved that his grandson thought he was good, and admired him for it. What could he do? Look into those warm brown eyes and say, "I am a selfish old rascal. I never did a good thing in my life, and I don't care about Earl's Court or the poor people"? He couldn't say that.

And so he called for Newick. They decided that they would tear down the horrible houses in Earl's Court and build new ones.

"It is Lord Fauntleroy who wants this," the earl told Newick. "You can tell the tenants that it was his idea."

It happened just as Mrs. Errol had hoped it would. Soon enough, workers had come to tear down the dirty cottages. Everyone in the village knew that little Lord Fauntleroy had helped them again.

If the boy only knew how they talked about him and praised him everywhere, how astonished he would have been! But he never realized. He lived his simple, happy life as usual. He played in the gardens. He read wonderful books and talked about them with the earl. He wrote long letters to Dick and to Mr. Hobbs. He rode his pony into town at his grandfather's side.

Cedric and the earl often rode over to Earl's Court together to watch the cottages being built. Cedric liked to learn about building and bricklaying. He asked many questions, and ended up making friends with all the workers.

When he left, the workers would talk about him. They would go home and tell their wives about him. And the women would tell one another. Soon, almost everyone in the village knew some story about little Lord Fauntleroy. And they knew that the "wicked earl" had found someone he cared for at last. Someone had finally warmed his bitter old heart.

But no one knew quite how much it had warmed. Day by day, the earl found himself caring more for his grandson, the only creature who had ever trusted him. The earl looked forward to the day the boy would grow up. He wondered what he'd become.

The boy can do anything! he would tell himself.

One evening, just before the Earl's Court cottages were finished, there was a grand dinner party at Dorincourt Castle. There had not been a dinner party there for a long time. The earl had even invited his sister, Lady Lorridaile. They hadn't spoken in many, many years. But when she and her husband received the invitation to go to the castle and meet the earl's heir, she couldn't resist.

Lady Lorridaile had heard a great many things about her brother over the years. She knew that he had paid very little attention to his children. And she knew how he had disliked them when they were older, especially the first two boys. She knew how ashamed of them he had been.

She had met only the earl's youngest son, Captain Errol. He had come to visit her on his own. Lady Lorridaile's kind heart had warmed through and through at the sight of him, and she had made him stay with her for a week. He was so sweet and light-hearted that she hoped to see him again. But when the earl found out about the stay, he told his son to never visit again.

Lady Lorridaile always remembered Captain Errol tenderly. She had heard about his marriage in New York and agreed that it was too quick, but she was very angry to hear that her brother had disowned him. Then came news of the captain's death. And then his two older brothers had died. And soon after came the story of the American child who had been brought to England to be Lord Fauntleroy. Lady Lorridaile had become even angrier when she learned how the earl treated the little Lord Fauntleroy's mother. It was a disgrace.

The stories of the kind, generous Lord Fauntleroy and what he had done for the people of Erlesboro had traveled far and wide. But when she met the boy himself, Lady Lorridaile discovered that he was even more delightful than the rumors had said he was.

She met him the morning of the dinner party, and said to him, "I am your aunt, Lady Lorridaile. And I loved your poor papa. You are just like him, do you know that?"

Cedric smiled, flushing slightly. "It makes me glad when people say that," he said. "Because it seems as if everyone liked him — just like Dearest."

Lady Lorridaile bent down and kissed the boy. From that moment, they were warm friends.

After meeting Cedric, Lady Lorridaile pulled the earl aside and said to him, "It could not possibly be better than this!"

"I think not," said the earl. "He is a fine little fellow. We are great friends. I will confess to you, I am in some slight danger of being rather an old fool about him."

"What does his mother think of you?" asked Lady Lorridaile.

"I have not asked her," said the earl, scowling.

"Well," said Lady Lorridaile, "I will be frank with you. I don't approve of what you're doing. I will be going to visit her today, before the party. If you wish to argue with me, do it now. What I hear of the young mother is that the child is lucky to have her. We have heard even at Lorridaile Park that your poorer tenants adore her already."

"They adore *him*," said the earl, nodding toward Cedric. "As to Mrs. Errol, you'll find her to be a pretty little woman. I'm rather in debt to her for giving some of her beauty to the boy. You may go see her if you like. All I ask is that she remain at Court Lodge, and that you not ask me to see her." Then he scowled again.

Lady Lorridaile went to visit Mrs. Errol right away. When she returned, she said to her brother, "She is the loveliest woman I ever saw! She has a voice like a silver bell. You may thank her for making the boy what he is. She has given him more than her beauty. You make a great mistake in not inviting her to live here."

But the earl didn't say a word.

That evening was the dinner party. Cedric was the center of attention. Everyone had something to say to him. They loved to hear him talk. He was so young, yet so serious about a great many worldly topics. The ladies petted him and asked him questions. The men asked him questions, too, and joked with him. Cedric thought the whole evening was delightful.

Even though everyone wanted to talk to him, Cedric still made time for his grandfather. More than once during the party, he went to stand beside the earl's chair.

The earl saw how the people noticed, and he smiled to himself. He knew what they were thinking. They were surprised that such a fine little boy obviously thought so highly of him. It pleased the earl to no end.

Mr. Havisham was supposed to be at the party, too, but he was late. Mr. Havisham was never, ever late. The earl found it quite strange. Mr. Havisham finally arrived just as the guests were about to go in to dinner.

He approached the earl before entering the

dining room. Mr. Havisham had an odd look on his face and was quite pale.

"I was delayed," Mr. Havisham said, "by an extraordinary event."

But there was no time to find out what the extraordinary event was. Dinner was served, and the earl sat down at the head of the table in front of his many guests. The earl noted that Mr. Havisham hardly ate a bite. He didn't smile, and he kept looking nervously over at Cedric.

Finally dinner ended and the guests moved to the drawing room.

Cedric followed, keeping up his talk with all his new friends. He had enjoyed himself so much that he wanted to stay up as late as he could. But soon, as he sat on the sofa and listened to the guests talk, his eyelids began to droop. He was quite sure he wasn't going to sleep, but there was a large yellow satin cushion behind him. His head

sank against the cushion, and his eyelids drooped
again. This time they stayed closed.

⁓

No sooner had the last guest left the room than
Mr. Havisham turned from his place by the fire.
He stepped nearer to the sofa. There was the little
Lord Fauntleroy, fast asleep. Mr. Havisham spent
a long moment staring at his pretty flushed face
and his tangled hair on the yellow cushion. He
had some strange and painful news to tell the
earl, and this sight made him not want to say it.

"Well, what is it?" demanded the earl's harsh
voice from behind Mr. Havisham. "What was the
extraordinary event?"

Mr. Havisham turned, rubbing his chin.

"It is bad news," he said. "The worst of news. I
am sorry to have to tell you."

The earl was feeling very nervous. "Why do

you look like that at the boy!" he said. "What does your news have to do with him?"

"My lord," started Mr. Havisham, "I will waste no words. My news has everything to do with the boy. And if we are to believe it, this is not Lord Fauntleroy who lies sleeping here on the sofa, but only the son of Captain Errol. The real Lord Fauntleroy is the child of your oldest son, Bevis, and is at this moment in a lodging-house in London."

The earl clutched the arms of his chair. His fierce old face was filled with rage.

"What do you mean?" he cried. "You lie!"

Mr. Havisham shook his head. "A woman came to see me this morning. She said Bevis married her six years ago in London. They had a bad argument a year after their marriage, and he paid her to stay away from him. She has a son who she says is Bevis's. She is an American of the lower class—an ignorant person—and until lately she did not understand what rights her son could claim as the heir to an earl. Then she met with a lawyer and found out that her son is really Lord Fauntleroy, heir to Dorincourt."

On the sofa, the boy sighed in his sleep.

The earl stared at his grandson. "I should refuse to believe a word of it," he said, "if it were not such ugly news. But it sounds a lot like my son Bevis. It is something Bevis would do. The woman is an uneducated person, you say?"

"I must admit that she cannot even spell her own name," said Mr. Havisham. "She cares only for the money."

The earl smiled bitterly.

"And I," he said, "I hated the other woman, the mother of this child. I refused to know her. And yet she can do far more than spell her own name. I suppose this is what I deserve."

Suddenly he sprang out of his chair and began to pace around the room. Fierce words poured from his lips. His rage and disappointment shook him the way a storm shakes a tree.

"I should have known!" he shrieked. He asked Mr. Havisham questions about the woman, about the proof. He kept pacing around the room. He turned first white and then purple with anger.

When at last he learned all there was to know, he looked terrible. "If anyone had told me I could grow to be fond of a child," he said, his voice shaking, "I would not have believed them."

He bent down and stood a minute or two looking at the happy, sleeping face. Then he turned away and rang the bell.

When the footman appeared, the earl pointed to the sofa.

"Take," he said, and then his voice changed a little, "take Lord Fauntleroy to his room."

CHAPTER 11

Anxiety in America

～๑～

When Mr. Hobbs's young friend left him to become Lord Fauntleroy, Mr. Hobbs became quite lonely. No one else came to his grocery store to chat the way Cedric had. No one else would read the newspapers with him. Or discuss politics. Or work on arithmetic while Mr. Hobbs added up his accounts.

At first, Mr. Hobbs just kept hoping that Cedric would come back. He kept expecting to see the boy standing in the doorway in his white suit, saying in his cheerful little voice, "Hallo, Mr.

Hobbs!" But as the days passed and this didn't happen, Mr. Hobbs began to feel very dull.

He didn't even enjoy his newspaper. He would read a little and then put it down, staring at the wall for a long time.

At night, when the store was closed, he would walk slowly until he reached the house where Cedric and his mother used to live. There was a sign on it that read HOUSE FOR RENT. Mr. Hobbs would stop near the sign and shake his head. After a while, he would walk back home, feeling gloomier than he had before.

This went on for weeks, until Mr. Hobbs remembered Cedric's other friend, the shoe-shine boy, Dick. Mr. Hobbs had never met Dick, but he felt that it was time. They were both friends of Cedric's. They had something in common.

So one day when Dick was hard at work shining a customer's boots, a short, stout man with a heavy face stopped on the sidewalk and stared at Dick's sign. It said:

PROFESSOR DICK TIPTON

CAN'T BE BEAT.

The man stared at the sign for so long, that when Dick was done with his customer, he asked if the man needed his shoes shined.

The stout man came forward and put his foot on the rest.

"Yes," he said. Once Dick started working, the man pointed to the sign and asked, "Where did you get that?"

"From a friend o' mine," said Dick. "A little feller. He's in England now. Gone back to be one o' those lords."

"Lord Fauntleroy—goin' to be the Earl of Dorincourt?" Mr. Hobbs asked.

Dick almost dropped his brush. "Do you know him?" he asked.

"I've known him," said Mr. Hobbs, "ever since he was born. We're lifetime friends, that's what we are."

He pulled the splendid gold watch out of his pocket and opened it so Dick could see what was carved inside. "When this you see, remember me," he read aloud.

They started talking about Cedric, now Lord Fauntleroy, living in England, and they couldn't stop. Dick said he was the nicest boy he had ever met. Mr. Hobbs said it was a pity they had to make an earl out of him, as he would have been perfect for the grocery business.

Soon enough, Mr. Hobbs decided that Dick should pay a visit to his store.

Dick was pleased about the visit. He had been a street kid nearly his whole life, but he had big plans. Someday he wanted to own a real business, like Mr. Hobbs did. So to be invited to visit a respectable man who owned a corner store, and even had a horse and wagon, seemed to him quite an event.

This was the beginning of a true friendship. Dick visited Mr. Hobbs more and more often, and they read newspaper articles about England. Mr. Hobbs was especially interested in anything having to do with earls.

They continued to write to Cedric, and Cedric wrote them back.

Mr. Hobbs and Dick found great pleasure in their letters. They talked them over and enjoyed every word. They spent days going over the letters they sent, and read them almost as often as the letters they received.

It was hard for Dick to write his letters. All his knowledge of reading and writing came from the short time he had lived with his older brother, Ben. He had never been to school with other children.

Dick told Mr. Hobbs all about his life with his

older brother, who had been good to him after their mother and father had died. Everything had been all right until Ben had married an awful girl named Minna. Minna was mad all the time. She yelled and screamed, and when she and Ben had a son, the baby did the same.

Ben finally left, going out West to set up a cattle ranch. Dick stayed with Minna, but she soon left, too—without even saying good-bye. People said that she and her baby had gone across the ocean to England. Dick didn't know whether this was true or not, but either way he ended up back on the streets with no one to help him.

But now he had a friend in Mr. Hobbs. He often told Mr. Hobbs stories of Minna and his brother. Ben had run into some bad luck out West and was now working at a ranch in California. It was very far away.

They were talking about this one day in Mr.

Hobbs's store when a letter was delivered by the postman. It was from Cedric!

Excited, Mr. Hobbs read it aloud:

Dorincourt Castle

My dear Mr. Hobbs, I write this in a great hurry because I have something curious to tell you. I know you will be very much surprised. It is all a mistake and I am not a lord and I shall not have to be an earl. There is a lady who was married to my uncle Bevis, who is dead, and she has a little boy and he is Lord Fauntleroy, because that is the way it is in England. Now my name is Cedric Errol like it was when I was in New York, and all the things will belong to the other boy. I thought at first I should have to give him my pony, but my grandfather says I need not. The lady brought her little boy to the castle and my grandfather was angry. I think she was angry, too, because she talked loudly. I never saw my grandfather angry before. I wish it did not make them all mad. I thought I would tell you and Dick right away, because you would be interested. So no more at present, with love from

Your Old Friend,

Cedric Errol (not Lord Fauntleroy)

Mr. Hobbs dropped the letter on the floor.

He was very upset. He had not liked the change to his young friend's life at first, but lately, he'd become all right with it. He might not have a good opinion of earls, but he thought Cedric would be a good one.

"They're trying to rob him!" he exclaimed.

When Dick left, Mr. Hobbs took a walk. He went to the empty house where Cedric and his mother used to live. He stood staring at the HOUSE FOR RENT sign for a long time, very, very disturbed.

CHAPTER 12

The Other Boy

❦

Everyone in the village and beyond had heard what happened to poor little Lord Fauntleroy. He was no longer Lord Fauntleroy, now that the other boy had been found. No one could stop talking about it.

At first, when the earl explained everything to Cedric, the little boy was very troubled.

"It makes me feel very strange," he told his grandfather. "Very strange."

The earl felt strange as well—stranger than he'd ever felt in his life.

"Will they take Dearest's house away from her—and her carriage?" asked Cedric in a rather unsteady voice.

"No!" the earl exclaimed. "They can take nothing from her."

Cedric looked at his grandfather with large, sad eyes. "The other boy," he said, his voice still shaking, "he will have to—to be your boy now—as I was—won't he?"

"No!" answered the earl. He said it so loudly that Cedric jumped.

"No?" Cedric said, confused. "Won't he? I thought—"

He stood up.

"Shall I be your boy, even if I'm not going to be an earl?" he asked. "Shall I be your boy, just as I was before?" His face was flushed, nervous about the answer.

"My boy!" the earl said, his voice now shaking. "Yes, you'll be my boy as long as I live. And by

George, sometimes I feel as if you were the only boy I ever had."

"Do you?" Cedric asked. "Well then, I don't care whether I am an earl or not. I thought— you see, I thought the one who was going to be the earl would have to be your boy, too, and— and I couldn't be. That was what made me feel so strange."

The earl put a hand on Cedric's shoulder.

"They shall take nothing from you. Not if I can help it," he said.

The earl hadn't realized how deep his fondness and pride in the boy had grown—until now. Looking at Cedric, it seemed impossible to the earl—impossible—to give up on the idea of him being Lord Fauntleroy. The earl had his heart set on it, and he would not give up without a fight.

A few days later, the lady who said she was the mother of the new Lord Fauntleroy visited Dorincourt Castle. The earl refused to see her.

Even the servants who saw her agreed that she was no "lady"—not the way Mrs. Errol was.

The earl didn't want to speak with her, but he knew he would have to sometime. Finally he went to see her at the Dorincourt Arms inn, where she was staying.

When she saw the old earl enter the room, she flew at him in a rage. She called him terrible names and said terrible things. She demanded all sorts of things from him—money for her son, and money for herself. She seemed to care only about the money she thought she was owed.

The earl simply stood there and let her scream. When she stopped, he said, "You say you are my eldest son's wife. If that is true, then the law is on your side and your boy is Lord Fauntleroy. But we will learn the truth. If what you say is true, I will provide for you. But I want to see nothing of you or the child for as long as I live. The castle will have enough of you after my death."

And then he turned his back on her and left.

A few days later, Mrs. Errol received a visitor. The maid looked excited. "It's the earl himself, ma'am," she said, almost trembling.

When Mrs. Errol entered the drawing room, she found a very tall, majestic-looking man waiting for her. He had a handsome, grim old face.

"Mrs. Errol, I believe?" he said.

"Yes," she replied.

"I am the Earl of Dorincourt," he said. He paused for a moment to look her over. "The boy looks very much like you."

"It has been often said so, my lord," she answered. "But I like to think that he looks like his father."

Her manner was direct, yet still sweet. She did not seem upset by the earl's sudden visit.

"Do you know why I have come here?" he asked.

"I have seen Mr. Havisham," said Mrs. Errol. "He has told me about the other boy——"

"That is what I have come to talk to you about," said the earl before she could finish. "We will look into it and find out if it is true. And whatever we can argue, we will argue. Your boy's rights——"

Now Mrs. Errol interrupted him. Her voice was very soft, but still strong.

"He must have nothing that does not rightfully belong to him."

"I suppose," the earl said, scowling slightly,

"that you do not want him to be the Earl of Dorincourt?"

She flushed.

"It is a very splendid thing to be the Earl of Dorincourt, my lord," she said. "I know that. But I care most that he should be what his father was—brave and honest, always."

"Not like his grandfather, eh?" the earl snapped.

"I have not had the pleasure of knowing his grandfather," said Mrs. Errol. "But I know my little boy believes—" She stopped speaking and looked quietly into his face. "I know that Cedric loves you."

"Would he have loved me," asked the earl, "if you had told him the truth about why you could not come to the castle?"

"No," Mrs. Errol said right away. "I think not. That was why I didn't wish him to know."

"Well," said the earl, "there are many women who would have told him."

He started to pace around the room.

"Yes, he is fond of me," he said, "and I am fond of him. I can't say I have ever been fond of anyone before. He has given me something to live for. I am proud of him, and I want him to be head of my family one day."

He came back and stood before Mrs. Errol.

"I am miserable," he said. "Miserable!"

And he looked as if he truly was. Even his pride could not keep his voice or hands from shaking. For a moment it seemed as if his deep, fierce eyes had tears in them.

"Perhaps it is because I am miserable that I have come to you," he said. He was almost glaring at her. "I used to hate you. I was jealous of you, but this awful business with the other woman and the other boy has changed that. I have been a stubborn old fool, and I have treated you badly. I know that. And now I am miserable. I came to you because you are like the boy. He cares for you, and I care for him. Treat me as well as you can, for Cedric's sake."

He spoke in a rough voice, but he was clearly hurting. Mrs. Errol was touched to the heart. She got up and moved an armchair forward.

"Please sit a moment," she said in a soft, caring voice. "You are not well."

He sat. She was so sweet to him, and he knew he didn't deserve it. He was grateful.

"Whatever happens," he said, "your boy will be taken care of. Now, and in the future."

"Thank you," Mrs. Errol replied.

"May I come to talk with you again?" he asked.

"As often as you wish, my lord," she said.

CHAPTER 13

Dick to the Rescue

❧

The story of Lord Fauntleroy and his problems soon made its way into the American newspapers.

One morning Dick was shining the shoes of one of his regular customers, a young lawyer named Mr. Harrison. The man knew that Dick liked to read news about England, so he gave him the paper when he was finished with it. That day he had an illustrated paper, with pictures of the people in the stories.

"Here's a paper for you," he said. "You should

learn about the nobility. Begin with the Right Honorable Earl of Dorincourt and Lady Fauntleroy. Their pictures are right here. Hallo! I say, Dick, what's the matter?"

The pictures he spoke of were on the front page. Dick was staring at them with his eyes and mouth wide open.

"What's wrong, Dick?" the lawyer asked again.

Dick pointed to the picture of a woman. Under it was written: "Mother (Lady Fauntleroy)." The woman had large eyes and black hair wound around her head. She was quite striking.

"I know her!" Dick exclaimed.

The young lawyer laughed. "Where did you meet her, Dick?" he asked. "When you ran over to Paris last week?"

Dick forgot to grin. He gathered his things and closed his business early for the day.

"Never mind," he said. "I know her!" He ran

off down the street to Mr. Hobbs's grocery store. He was out of breath by the time he reached the counter.

"Hallo!" Mr. Hobbs exclaimed. "What have you got there?"

"Look!" Dick panted. "Look at the woman in the picture. *She* ain't no Lady Fauntleroy. That's Minna! I'd know her anywhere."

Mr. Hobbs dropped into his seat.

"I knew it was a put-on job," he said. "I knew someone was cheating him."

Dick and Mr. Hobbs looked at each other, trying to figure out what to do.

Then Dick had an idea. "Say," he said, "that feller who gave me the paper—he's a lawyer. Wouldn't you say that's what we need now, a lawyer? To prove she isn't who she says she is?"

Mr. Hobbs was impressed. "That's so!" he exclaimed. "This here calls for lawyers."

And so Mr. Hobbs closed up his shop and

marched with Dick to the office where the lawyer, Mr. Harrison, worked.

Mr. Harrison believed Dick to be an honest kid, but if he had not been a new lawyer, hungry to start his career, he may have laughed at the boy and told him to leave. But Mr. Harrison had nothing to lose and everything to gain.

"Well," he said, "no harm can be done by looking into it. There have already been some questions about the child. The woman's story keeps changing. The first people to write to are Dick's brother and the Earl of Dorincourt's lawyer."

Before the sun went down that day, two letters had been written and sent in two different directions. One was speeding to England. The other was on a train headed for California. The first was addressed to "T. Havisham, Esq." and the second to "Benjamin Tipton."

CHAPTER 14

The Exposure

⌒

It is astonishing how quickly everything can change. It took only a few minutes for the little boy on the stool in Mr. Hobbs's grocery store to learn that he was no ordinary boy, but rather an English lord. And it took only a few minutes for him to become an ordinary boy again. And surprising as it may appear, it took only that long to make him a lord once more.

The woman who called herself Lady Fauntleroy was not too clever. She couldn't keep her story straight when Mr. Havisham asked her questions about how old her son was and where he was born. There seemed to be no doubt that she had been married to Bevis, and that they had argued and she had been paid to stay away from him. But there was much doubt about the boy.

Then the letter from America arrived.

Soon enough, there was a knock on the woman's door and Mr. Havisham entered. With him were three people. One was a sharp-faced young boy. The other was a tall young man. And the third was the Earl of Dorincourt.

The woman sprang to her feet and cried out in terror. She looked very upset.

Dick grinned a little when he saw her. "Hallo, Minna!" he said.

The tall young man—Ben—stood very still. He just looked at her.

"Do you know her?" Mr. Havisham asked.

"Yes," said Ben. "I know her, and she knows me." And he turned his back on her and went to stand by the window, as if he hated the sight of her.

The woman flew into a rage. There was no denying the truth now.

Suddenly Ben turned away from the window.

"Where is the child?" he demanded. "He's going with me!"

As he finished saying those words, the bedroom door opened and a little boy looked in. Everyone could see how much he looked like Ben.

Ben walked up to him and took his hand. His own hand was trembling.

"I'm your father, Tom," he said to the little boy. "I've come to take you away. Where's your hat?"

The boy pointed to where it lay on a chair. He seemed pleased to hear that he was going away.

Ben took the hat and marched to the door.

"If you want me again," he told Mr. Havisham, "you know where to find me."

provide for Dick and give him a good, solid education. And so Dick was sent away to school.

And Mr. Hobbs, after spending time with Cedric and touring the castle and learning the history of all things that made lords into earls, softened a little on his view about the British royalty.

Privately, Mr. Hobbs found that he was not so disgusted with earls as he used to be. He ended up staying for a long time at the Dorincourt Arms, visiting his young friend often. Then, to the great surprise of Cedric and everyone else who knew Mr. Hobbs, he decided to stay in England for good.

He sold his shop in New York and opened another one in Erlseboro. The place became quite popular, since people from the castle shopped there all the time.

Finally the day came when Cedric turned eight years old. All the lords and ladies were invited to his party, and everyone from the village, too. What a grand day it was, and how his young lordship enjoyed it!

How beautiful the park looked, filled with people dressed in their colorful best. Flags were flying from the top of the castle. So many people were there, under the trees and in the tents and on the lawns. There were farmers and farmers' wives in their best clothes, and girls and their sweethearts, and children chasing one another about. And at the castle there were ladies and gentlemen who had come to see the fun. Lady Lorridaile was there, thrilled at the turn of events.

Cedric was thrilled, too. His Dearest was with him, and everyone seemed so happy to celebrate his birthday. The sun shone and the flags fluttered and the games were played and the dances danced.

The people had a toast for his birthday, and Cedric stood and smiled. He bowed, flushing rosy red up to the roots of his bright hair.

"Is it because they like me, Dearest?" he asked Mrs. Errol. "Is it, Dearest? I'm so glad!"

And then the earl put a hand on his shoulder and said to him, "Cedric, tell them that you thank them for their kindness."

Cedric glanced at his mother.

"Must I?" he asked shyly.

His mother nodded and smiled. So he stood and, with a very brave face, he spoke out in his ringing, childish voice.

"Thank you so much!" he said. "And—I hope you'll enjoy my birthday—because I've enjoyed it so much. And I'm very glad I'm going to be an earl. I didn't think at first I should like it, but now I do—and—and when I am an earl, I will try to be as good as my grandfather."

People shouted and clapped, and Cedric stepped back with a sigh of relief. He put his hand into the earl's hand and stood close to him, leaning against his side.

The whole world seemed beautiful to him.

Someone else was just as happy: an old man who — though he had been rich and noble all his life — had not honestly been very happy before this.

The earl loved Cedric. And he found that every day he was more and more pleased with the boy's mother. He liked to hear her gentle voice and see her sweet face. He liked to watch her when he sat in his armchair. He saw her with her son, and listened as she talked to him. He heard the loving words she used with her child, words the earl couldn't recall ever hearing before. He began to see why the little fellow who had lived on a New York side street, and had known grocerymen and made friends with shoe-shine boys, was so well-bred. No one could be ashamed of him.

It was really a very simple thing, after all. It was only that the little boy had lived near a kind and gentle heart. He had been taught to always think kind thoughts, and to care for others. It is a very little thing, perhaps, but it is the best thing of all. The boy had known nothing of earls and castles. He had hardly known about grand and splendid things. But he had always been loved because he was kind and loving. And to be so is like being born a king.

What Do *You* Think?
Questions for Discussion

࿊

Have you ever been around a toddler who keeps asking the question "Why?" Does your teacher call on you in class with questions from your homework? Do your parents ask you questions about your day at the dinner table? We are always surrounded by questions that need a specific response. But is it possible to have a question with no right answer?

The following questions are about the book you just read. But this is not a quiz! They are designed to help you look at the people, places, and events in the story from different angles. These questions do not have specific answers. Instead, they might make you think of the story in a completely new way.

Think carefully about each question and enjoy discovering more about this classic story.

1. The clearest memory Cedric has of his father is being carried on his shoulders. Do you have a favorite memory with either of your parents?

2. Cedric learns to read when he is very little. How old were you when you learned to read? Do you have a favorite book?

3. How do Cedric's friends feel when they learn that he is moving to England? Have any of your friends ever moved away?

4. How does Cedric react when he learns that he will one day be an earl? How would you feel if you suddenly found out you were royalty?

5. Cedric tells Dick that he's in danger of becoming an earl when he grows up. Why does he see this as a bad thing? What do you want to be when you grow up?

6. Cedric says that if he had a lot of money, he would help his poorer friends. What would you do if you suddenly had a lot of money?

7. How does Cedric react when his aunt says that his is just like his papa? Who would you most like to be like?

8. Why does Cedric want to stay up late after the dinner party? What is the latest you've ever stayed up?

9. How does Minna react when her secret is exposed? Were you surprised to find out the truth? Has anyone ever caught you in a lie?

10. Why does Mr. Hobbs decide to move to England? If you could live anywhere, where would it be?

Afterword

By Arthur Pober, Ed.D.

༄

First impressions are important.

Whether we are meeting new people, going to new places, or picking up a book unknown to us, first impressions count for a lot. They can lead to warm, lasting memories or can make us shy away from any future encounters.

Can you recall your own first impressions and earliest memories of reading the classics?

Do you remember wading through pages and pages of text to prepare for an exam? Or were you the child who hid under the blanket to read with a flashlight, joining forces with Robin Hood to save Maid Marian? Do you remember only how long it took you to read a lengthy novel such as *Little Women*? Or did you become best friends with the March sisters?

Even for a gifted young reader, getting through long chapters with dense language can easily become overwhelming and can obscure the richness of the story and its characters. Reading an abridged, newly crafted version of a classic novel can be the gentle introduction a child needs to explore the characters and story-line without the frustration of difficult vocabulary and complex themes.

Reading an abridged version of a classic novel gives the young reader a sense of independence and the satisfaction of finishing a "grown-up" book. And when a child is engaged with and inspired by a classic story, the tone is set for further exploration of the story's themes, characters, history, and details. As a child's reading skills advance, the desire to tackle the original, unabridged version of the story will naturally emerge.

If made accessible to young readers, these stories can become invaluable tools for understanding themselves in the context of their families and social environments. This is why the Classic Starts series includes questions that stimulate discussion regarding the impact and social relevance of the characters and stories today. These questions can foster lively conversations between children and their parents or teachers. When we look at the issues, values, and standards of past times in terms of how we live now, we can appreciate literature's classic tales in a very personal and engaging way.

Share your love of reading the classics with a young child, and introduce an imaginary world real enough to last a lifetime.

Dr. Arthur Pober, Ed.D.

Dr. Arthur Pober has spent more than twenty years in the fields of early childhood and gifted education. He is the former principal of one of the world's oldest laboratory schools for gifted youngsters, Hunter College Elementary School, and former Director of Magnet Schools for the Gifted and Talented for more than 25,000 youngsters in New York City.

Dr. Pober is a recognized authority in the areas of media and child protection and is currently the U.S. representative to the European Institute for the Media and European Advertising Standards Alliance.

Explore these wonderful stories in our
Classic Starts™ library.